D0188138

HENRY HECKELBECK

Builds a Robot

By **Wanda Coven**

Illustrated by **Priscilla Burris**

LITTLE SIMON

New York   London   Toronto   Sydney   New Delhi

LITTLE SIMON
An imprint of Simon & Schuster Children's Publishing Division
1230 Avenue of the Americas, New York, New York 10020
First Little Simon paperback edition January 2022
Copyright © 2022 by Simon & Schuster, Inc.
Also available in a Little Simon hardcover edition.
All rights reserved, including the right of reproduction in whole or in part in any form. LITTLE SIMON is a registered trademark of Simon & Schuster, Inc., and associated colophon is a trademark of Simon & Schuster, Inc.
For information about special discounts for bulk purchases, please contact Simon & Schuster Special Sales at 1-866-506-1949 or business@simonandschuster.com. The Simon & Schuster Speakers Bureau can bring authors to your live event. For more information or to book an event contact the Simon & Schuster Speakers Bureau at 1-866-248-3049 or visit our website at www.simonspeakers.com.
Designed by Leslie Mechanic
Manufactured in the United States of America 1221 MTN
10 9 8 7 6 5 4 3 2 1
Library of Congress Cataloging-in-Publication Data
Names: Coven, Wanda, author. | Burris, Priscilla, illustrator.
Title: Henry Heckelbeck builds a robot / by Wanda Coven ; illustrated by Priscilla Burris. | Description: First Little Simon paperback edition. | New York : Little Simon, 2022. | Series: Henry Heckelbeck ; 8 | Summary: Henry Heckelbeck builds a robot for class, but when he uses magic to put the gears together, his robot is a little more than he can handle. | Identifiers: LCCN 2021027602 (print) | LCCN 2021027603 (ebook) | ISBN 9781665911375 (paperback) | ISBN 9781665911382 (hardcover) | ISBN 9781665911399 (ebook)
Subjects: CYAC: Robots—Fiction. | Magic—Fiction. | Classification: LCC PZ7.C83393 Ho 2022 (print) | LCC PZ7.C83393 (ebook) | DDC [Fic]—dc23
LC record available at https://lccn.loc.gov/2021027602
LC ebook record available at https://lccn.loc.gov/2021027603

CONTENTS

Chapter 1

A SPECIAL PROJECT

Henry Heckelbeck was thrilled because it was Friday. And Friday meant no homework until Monday. *Woooo!*

Then his teacher, Ms. Mizzle, made an announcement.

She said, "Class, I am going to assign a very *special* science project!"

Henry looked over at his best friend, Dudley Day. Both boys knew "special project" meant "homework." And they were both right.

Ms. Mizzle smiled. "I think you'll like this one. We are going to build robots!"

The class gasped, and everyone began talking until Ms. Mizzle whistled through her fingers. The class buzz stopped.

"You have one week to build your robot," she said.

"Can we make the robot however we want?" asked Adia Ackers.

Ms. Mizzle nodded. "Yes! Use any materials you'd like. Have fun! Be creative!"

Dudley raised his hand. "May we even use CANDY?"

"And Popsicle sticks?" asked somebody else.

"What if we wanted to make an animal robot?" blurted another student.

Ms. Mizzle laughed. "Yes to *all* your questions!"

The bell rang. Chairs scraped across the floor.

"Get started this weekend!" Ms. Mizzle called over the noise. "And we will talk about your plans on Monday."

Henry and Dudley walked to their cubbies.

"I might make a soccer ball robot," said Dudley. "What about you?"

Henry shrugged. "I'm not sure yet."

The boys grabbed their backpacks and gave each other a high five.

The weekend had officially begun!

Chapter 2

NO BOT

When Henry got home, he kicked off his shoes and dropped his backpack with a thump.

I should make a robot to put my stuff away! he thought.

"Hi, Henry!" called Mom.

She was sitting with his sister, Heidi, at the kitchen table. They were working on something.

"Mom got us a new family puzzle," Heidi said.

Mom held up a pirate puzzle box. "Arr, help us find the edges, matey!"

Henry sat down and picked
through the pieces.

Suddenly Dad walked in with
takeout from Burger Burgers.

It was one of Henry's favorite
restaurants.

"Who wants to have burgers
for Friday Night Movie Night?"
Dad cheered.

Everyone did! So Henry grabbed a plate and thought, *Tomorrow. I'll work on my robot project tomorrow.*

Cheereep! Cha-deep!

Sparrows sang outside Henry's window. His eyes winked open as he sat up and yawned. Ribbons of sunlight streamed across his blanket.

It's robot time! he thought.

Then Henry's bedroom door
creaked open. It was Heidi.
"Dad made WAFFLES!"
Clunk! She shut the door and
then cracked it open again.
"With WHIPPED CREAM!"

Clunk! She shut the door again and then cracked it open again.

"But he BROKE the toaster!"

As the sweet smell of waffles seeped into the room, Henry's belly rumbled.

"I can't build a robot on an empty stomach!" he said out loud.

Henry bolted downstairs to the kitchen, where Dad set waffles onto plates and swirled whipped cream over everything.

"So, I have to build a robot for school!" Henry said as he sat at the table.

"What kind?" Dad asked.

Henry licked the back of his fork. "One that will fly me around the WORLD!"

Heidi laughed. "How long do you have to build it?" she asked.

"Um, one week," Henry said before taking a big bite.

Heidi raised an eyebrow. "Good luck with THAT!"

Mom rested her hand on Henry's shoulder. "I'm sure you'll find the perfect robot idea," she said, "but you'll have to find it outside. It's too nice a day to spend inside."

So after breakfast Henry played soccer in the backyard with his sister. Then they cleaned the playhouse, ate lunch, and read books in the shade.

When the day finally turned
to night, Henry hadn't thought
about robot ideas at all.

Chapter 3

STILL NO BOT

Today is the day I start my ROBOT project! Henry told himself on Sunday morning.

But Aunt Trudy had other plans. She sailed in the back door with a bag of groceries.

"Brunch is here!" she sang as her red braid swished behind her. "I'm making eggs Benedict!"

Then she pulled out a board game. "And while I'm cooking, we'll play Candy Rush!"

Oh yeah, Henry thought. Brunch and board games had become a Sunday tradition at the Heckelbeck house. How could he forget?

Candy Rush was like Bingo with candy. If you match five candies in a row, you win.

Aunt Trudy shuffled the cards as the others took their candy boards.

As she read each card aloud,
Aunt Trudy also kept cooking
brunch. Of course, it helped
that she was magic.

Henry and Heidi were tied
with four candy matches.
Aunt Trudy said, "Time-out,
everyone! Brunch is served!"

The plates floated over to
the table, and the family sat
down to eat.

After brunch Aunt Trudy took Henry and Heidi to their favorite toy store, The Enchanted Forest. She bought them each a fortune-telling fish. The kids placed the thin plastic red fish on the palms of their hands.

"Look! The fish's head and tail are curling!" cried Henry.

Heidi looked at the key to the fortune-telling fish. "That means you're in LOVE."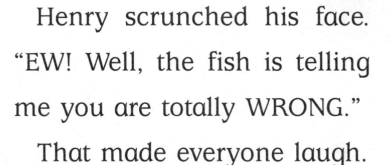

Henry scrunched his face. "EW! Well, the fish is telling me you are totally WRONG."

That made everyone laugh.

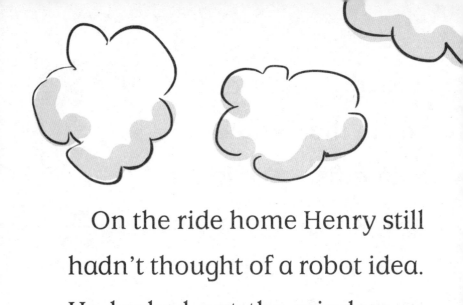

On the ride home Henry still hadn't thought of a robot idea. He looked out the window.

"Look! That cloud looks like a robot!" he cried.

Heidi rolled her eyes. "Have you even started your robot project?"

"No," Henry said quietly. "Not unless you count the robot cloud."

Aunt Trudy looked at Henry in her rearview mirror. "When you get home, take some quiet time," she said. "The idea will come to you, I'm sure."

Henry slid down in his seat
and said, "I sure hope so."

Chapter 4

MEGABOT

Henry sat on his bed that night and listened for ideas. He wondered what they would sound like. Would they be loud or quiet? Then . . . *Pippity! Pop!* His ideas danced like popcorn!

A bubble gum machine robot.

A robot that lays golden eggs.

A cloud robot that tells the future.

A tiny robot for ants.

A dog-walking robot.

Henry couldn't settle on one idea. Each new idea always seemed better than the last. So Henry thought and thought until he fell asleep.

The next morning Henry hopped on the bus *without* a robot idea.

Dudley waved him over to their seat.

"Henry! Check out what I did ALL weekend!" Dudley cheered.

He pulled out a cardboard robot from his backpack. It had a square head, a rectangular body, and empty toilet paper rolls for legs. A yellow thunderbolt zigzagged across the robot's body.

"Meet MEGABOT!" said Dudley as if he were introducing a *real* superhero.

Henry's eyes grew wide. "Whoa! That is SO cool!"

"Thanks!" said Dudley. "It's still in the planning stage. The final MEGABOT will be WAY better."

Henry gulped and thought, *Wow, Dudley worked on his robot ALL weekend. Does that mean EVERYBODY in my class worked on their robot project this weekend?*

He sure hoped not.

Chapter 5

ULTRA-GOAL BOT

Merg, thought Henry as he walked into the classroom.

Everybody had a robot plan. Ms. Mizzle even had students come to her desk and talk about their robots.

Henry slumped in his chair so Ms. Mizzle wouldn't notice him. And it worked! Soon the bell rang for lunch and recess.

"Want to come over after school?" asked Dudley as they swung on the swings. "I have a new video game we can play!"

"I can't," said Henry. "I have to work on my robot idea. Do you think Max has one yet?"

"Just ask her!" said Dudley. "She's right over there!"

Henry spied Max kicking a soccer ball.

"Hey, MAX!" Henry shouted, waving to her.

Max juggled the ball over to the swings. "What's up?"

Henry and Dudley dragged their shoes on the dirt to slow down.

"Do you have a robot idea
yet?" asked Henry.

Max laughed. "Of course I
do! Don't YOU?"

Henry jerked his swing to a
stop. "No, not yet."

Max pulled a paper out of her back pocket and unfolded it. "This is my ULTRA-GOAL BOT," she said. "It shoots soccer balls to train goalies like us!"

Henry hopped off the swing
and looked more closely.

"Wow, that's really cool!" he admitted.

Max nodded. Then she smirked and said, "You know, you're, like, the only kid who hasn't started your robot project."

She was right. And Henry wasn't excited about it.

Chapter 6

ME BOT?

Henry raced to his bedroom after school. He yanked open his desk drawers and started pulling out stuff, looking for something to spark a good robot idea.

He found three lucky rocks,
a plastic dinosaur, and neon-
green clapper hands.
Maybe they could
be robot parts?
Henry stacked
his lucky rocks on
top of each other.
Then he placed the
plastic dinosaur on
top with the clappers as hands,
but the tower collapsed.

And so did Henry. He flopped
flat onto his back.

"Building a robot is TOO
hard!" he complained.

Suddenly a strange glowing light caught his eye. It was that old magic book!

"MAGIC is JUST what I need!" cried Henry as the book floated over to him.

The medallion rose into the
air and came to rest
around Henry's neck.

Swoosh!

The magic book
opened, and the
pages began to flutter
until they found the right spell.

Build a Bit-of-You Robot

(For wizards who need a helping hand.)

Have you ever dreamed about building your own robot? What if your robot was programmed to clean your room? Or make treats for you? Or even help with your homework? If this sounds like your kind of robot, then this is the spell for you!

Ingredients:
1 favorite book
1 of your T-shirts
1 broken toaster
1 large handful of
   nuts and bolts

gather the ingredients together in a pile. Hold your medallion in your left hand, and place your right hand over the mix. Chant the following spell:

A little bit of you!

A little MORE of you!

Mix it all together in a robot brew!

Say the magic words: one, two, three!

Robot! Robot! Come to me!

Robot stays until no longer needed.
Lessons not included.

Henry helped himself to
a handful of nuts and bolts
from Dad's workbench. Next
he found the broken toaster in
the garage.

Then Henry snuck everything back to his bedroom and piled it on the floor.

He tossed a soccer T-shirt and a favorite book on top of the mix. Then he grabbed his medallion and chanted the spell. *WHOOSH!* A strong gust of wind swept through his room. Henry shut his eyes. When the wind stopped, he slowly opened them back up.

72

There, in the magical mist,
stood a shadowy figure.

Chapter 7

HENBOT!

"Hello, Henry!" said a kid-size robot.

Henry jumped backward. He couldn't believe his eyes. "Whoa! You look like ME if I were made of metal."

The robot had wheels instead of feet. It rolled toward Henry slowly.

"Correct," he said. "I look like you because I am your HenBot. I am programmed to know everything about you!"

"Everything?" Henry asked. "Like what?"

Blip! Bleep! Blurrrp! chirped HenBot, with colorful blinking lights.

Then HenBot said, "Henry Heckelbeck is a soccer goalie and a super spy! His favorite colors are blue and red. Your best friend is Dudley Day. And right now you are surprised."

Henry pinched himself to make sure he wasn't dreaming.

"How did you know all that?" he asked.

HenBot giggled. "Because I'm a *magic* robot, silly! Now, would you like to play a game?"

A door flipped open on HenBot's body, and out popped a mechanical arm holding a soccer ball.

Henry clapped his hands.
"Yes! Let's play!"

First they played hide-and-seek. Then they played the Floor Is Lava. Then they invented a game called Soccer-Dodge-and-Seek.

Henry loved his new robot, but there was one problem: HenBot was too good to be true!

Would anybody at school believe Henry had made *this*?

Chapter 8

PUZZLED

The next day HenBot was wearing Henry's backpack.

"I am ready for school!" HenBot said.

"Hmm," said Henry. "Why don't you stay here instead?"

"Okay," HenBot said as he gave Henry the backpack. "I made your favorite lunch."

Henry opened it up to find the perfect pizza inside. It smelled great.

"Thanks, HenBot!" he said. "I'll be home soon. Promise!"

Dudley was not bouncing on the bus seat when Henry slid next to him.

"Ugh, MEGABOT is a mega failure," Dudley moaned.

"But it looked so COOL!" said Henry.

Dudley hung his head. "It LOOKS cool, but it can't DO anything cool! It needs lasers or rockets . . . and we don't have those at my house."

Henry nodded. Lasers and rockets *were* hard to find.

"How's your robot coming along?" Dudley asked.

Henry frowned. "Let's just say I'm having robot problems of my own."

Max was sitting on the steps, waiting for her friends.

"Hey, Max! How's your ULTRA-GOAL BOT?" asked Henry.

"Not great," she said. "I tried to make it life-size, but it came out small."

Henry held out a hand and pulled Max to her feet.

"It's still a really good idea," he said.

Max groaned. "It is if you want to goalie-train MICE."

As the three friends walked, Henry thought, *HenBot is definitely too high-tech for school. Why would the magic book cast a spell to create something I can't use?*

Chapter 9

UNPUZZLED

Henry couldn't believe his eyes when he got home.

"Whoa! What did you DO to my room?" he asked.

HenBot bleeped cheerfully. "I cleaned it top to bottom!"

Henry's games had been put away. His books were in alphabetical order. Even the cobweb on his ceiling fan was gone.

Only one thing was out: Henry's jigsaw puzzles. And they were all put together!

"Aww, why did you finish my puzzles?" Henry asked.

"They were broken," said HenBot. "So I fixed them. Should I break them again? I am here to help you, after all."

Suddenly Henry snapped his fingers. The robot mystery was solved.

HenBot wasn't meant to *be* his robot project. He was here to *help*!

"I need a favor," Henry said. "Will you help me build a robot for school?"

HenBot lit up. "Yes. I would love to."

Henry looked at his puzzles and had a great idea. Before he could say anything, HenBot beamed a robot plan onto the wall. And it was exactly what Henry had been thinking about!

"Cool!" said Henry.

They got right to work building the robot. Henry gave orders, and HenBot repeated each order and then carried it out.

"Popsicle sticks!"

"Popsicle sticks!"

"Glue!"

"Glue!"

"Googly eyes!"

"Googly eyes!"

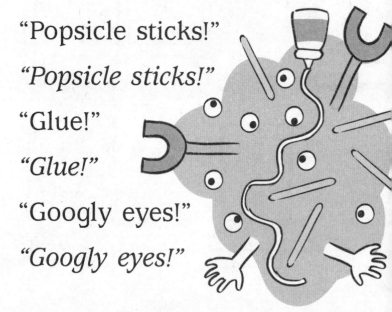

"More glue!"

"More glue!"

"Wire cutters!"

"Wire cutters!"

When it was done, Henry declared, "It's a masterpiece!"

"Correct," agreed HenBot.
"And now I must go!"

Henry felt a little sad. "But will I ever see you again?"

HenBot beeped. "Of course! I'm magic, silly. You'll see me when you *need* me."

Henry hugged HenBot. Then *WHOOSH!* The robot was gone.

Chapter 10

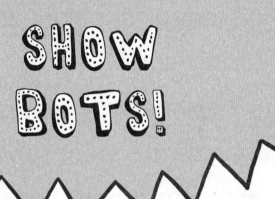

SHOW BOTS!

On Friday, Henry's classroom was filled with robots. Ryan Riley got to present his first.

He had made a hockey-player robot called the Puck Monster!

Ryan set his robot on a table in front of the class. It held a hockey stick.

"He shoots! He scores!" cried Ryan as the robot shot a mini puck into a mini hockey net.

Nina Noff went next. "One time I got in trouble for bringing my Boogie Bot to school," she said. "But it's OKAY to have a dancing robot in class now. Meet the Dancing Queen!"

Music rang out as Nina switched on her robot, and it spun, shook, and twirled.

"Dance along with us!" cried Nina, and the whole class boogied—even Ms. Mizzle.

Then Max walked to the head of the class. Her robot was hidden under a white cloth.

"Introducing . . . ULTRA-GOAL BOT!" said Max as she whipped off the cloth. "She can kick a ball past anyone! See if you can stop ULTRA-GOAL BOT!"

Max shifted the robot toward the class and placed a mini soccer ball in front of it. The kids held up their hands as the robot kicked the ball. Henry caught the ball in midair, and everyone clapped.

"Nice save, Henry!" said Ms. Mizzle. "Why don't you go next?"

Henry tossed the ball back to Max. Then he carried his robot and a tray to the front of the class.

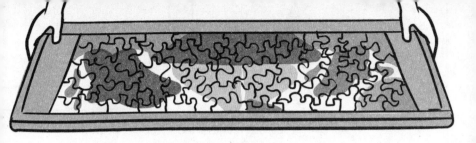

"Here we have a finished jigsaw puzzle," Henry began. "Everybody likes to put puzzles TOGETHER. But who likes to take them APART?"

The class shouted their answers.

"Not me!"

"Me neither!"

Henry held his robot up, and the class quieted down.

"Meet the Puzzle Buster!" said Henry as he put the robot by the puzzle and pressed a button.

The robot lifted the puzzle up like a forklift, and the pieces broke apart.

The class cheered wildly for
Henry.

"Would you make a Puzzle
Buster for our
classroom?" asked
Ms. Mizzle. "We
could sure use one!"

Henry's face lit up. "Of course I will!"

And this time Henry didn't mind doing extra homework, because it meant he'd get to work with HenBot again.

And *that* was totally magical.

Check out the next book

Henry Heckelbeck wriggled from under his covers and gazed at the twinkly stars. He heard Dad's slippers *wisp* down the hallway. They stopped in front of Henry's door.

An excerpt from *Henry Heckelbeck Is Out of This World*

"Too excited to sleep?" Dad asked.

Henry turned around. "Yup, way too excited!" he said.

In the morning Henry's class was going on a field trip to the Space Center, which had rocket ships and maybe even *aliens*.

"Have you ever been to space, Dad?" Henry asked.

Dad sat down and said, "Only in my dreams."

An excerpt from *Henry Heckelbeck Is Out of This World*

Henry crawled under the covers as Dad handed him a stuffed green alien.

"Maybe you'll space travel in your dreams tonight," Dad said.

Henry yawned. "If I ever fall asleep."

Dad pushed Henry's hair out of his eyes. "Pretend you're sleeping in space," he said.

An excerpt from *Henry Heckelbeck Is Out of This World*